SHADOWS OF THE ENCRYPTED

NITYA NAIR MALAPIL

Contents

Contents

Preface

Writing the triplet's adventure was a journey of creativity and exploration. Inspired by my love of mystery and companionship, this novel grew out of a childhood filled with stories of surprise and inquiry. I hope you enjoy reading it as much as I did creating it.

So Welcome to this amazing adventure. This work came from my interest in mystery and the persistent power of friendship. Describing my personal experiences and a passion for writing, I created this novel to take readers to a realm where bravery meets curiosity. Join Derek, Evan, and Alyssa on their thrilling voyage, allowing your imagination to fly with each page turn.

Nitya N Malapil
Author

Dr. Philosopher

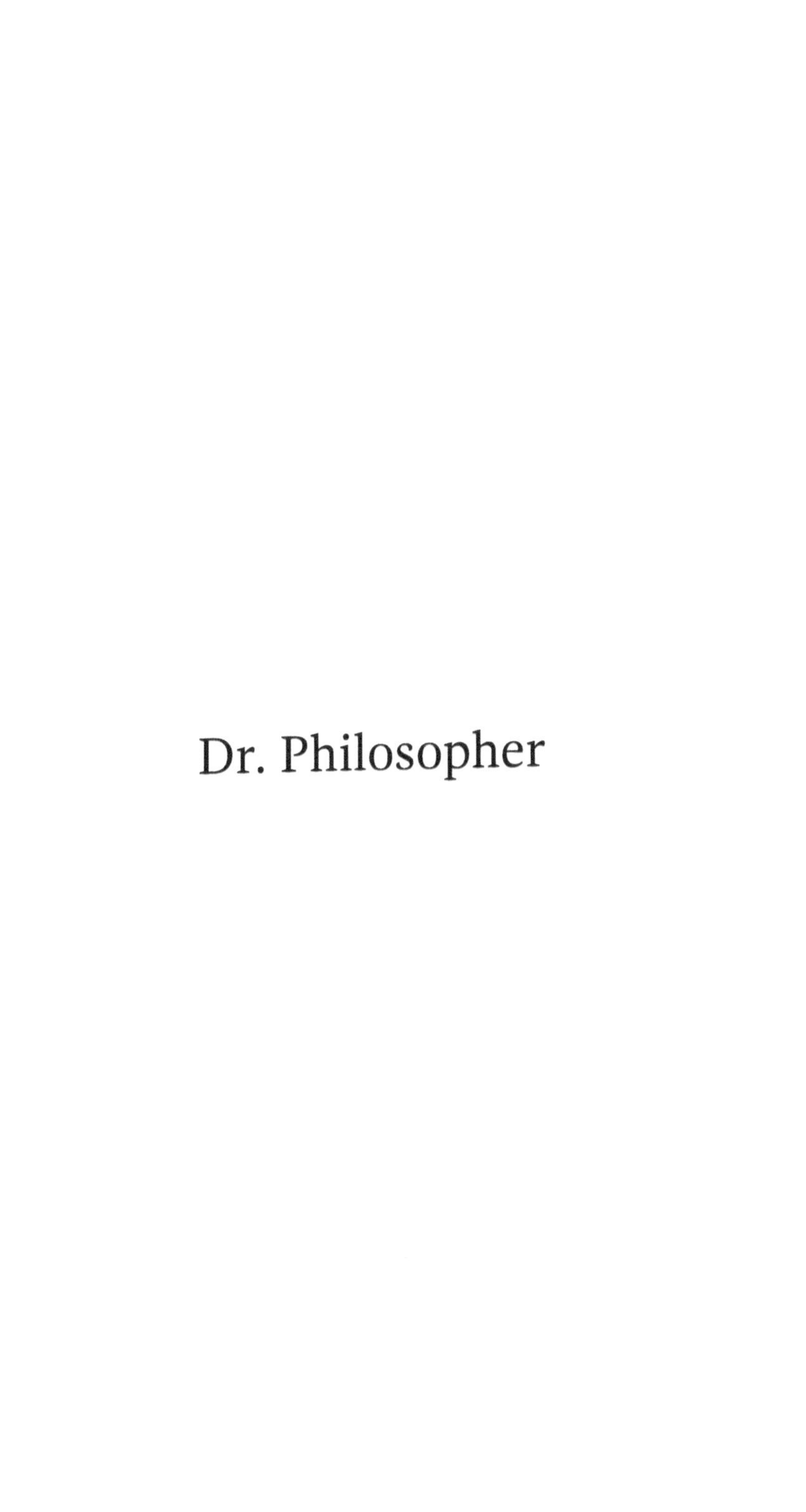

CHAPTER I

The Sudden Disappearance

The story begins with a modest cottage residence on the outskirts of town. Derek, Evan, and Alyssa, the triplets, were turning sixteen in a week. Except for Alyssa, the lads were excited about their birthday. She had no choice but to share it with her annoying brothers. She wanted a beautiful birthday celebration in which she would be treated like a VIP.

The parents then went out to get some decorations for their birthday party. All their friends, including their best friend Dr. Philosopher, were invited. He's a tall man with grey hair (at times, he reminded of Albert Einstein), a thin mustache, and a frightening look, but he's a lovely guy, else we wouldn't be friends with him, would we?

When the big day arrived, the triplets were overjoyed at the idea of their coming birthday party. That night, Alyssa was unable to sleep. Not because of the exactment of their party but she had been hearing noises in the backyard. While they were accompanied their mother in putting up the decorations, Alyssa had a nagging feeling that something was not right. Dr. Phil (as he is known) has not yet arrived at their home.

Dr. Phill was a solitary man with no family. He would always show up at their front door in the morning to have some fun with them. Today had already been an interesting day, and she wanted to find out more. She, along with Derek and Evan, had to lie to their parents since they would not let them investigate.

The triplets made their way to his residence through the back alley. When they arrived, the main door was wide open. Then it hit Alyssa. The noise, the nightmare, the creaky noises from the backyard were coming from his house. He had been KIDNAPPED.

CHAPTER II

The Investigation Begins

The triplets stood in shock at the open door of Dr. Phil's house. Alyssa's heart raced, but Derek and Evan were more excited than scared. This was an adventure they could not resist. They tiptoed inside, trying not to make a sound.

The house was a mess. Papers were scattered everywhere, and it looked like there had been a struggle. Evan picked up a crumpled piece of paper. "Look at this," he whispered, holding up what looked like a map with strange markings.

Alyssa examined it closely. "This could be a clue," she said, her eyes widening. "But we need to be careful. Whoever took Dr. Phil might come back."

Derek nodded, already thinking of how they could use this situation to their advantage. "We should split up and look for more clues," he suggested. "I'll check the living room, Evan can take the kitchen, and Alyssa can look upstairs."

Alyssa hesitated. "I don't want to go alone," she admitted. "What if the kidnapper is still here?"

Evan grinned. "Don't worry, Alyssa. If we stick together, we will be fine. Plus, I bet the kitchen has snacks."

They started their search, trying to make as little noise as possible. In the living room, Derek found a peculiar book with a hidden compartment. Inside was a small vial of glowing liquid. "What do you think this is?" he wondered aloud.

Meanwhile, in the kitchen, Evan discovered a half-written note on the counter. It was from Dr. Phil, mentioning something about a "secret formula" and "the key to everything."

Alyssa, who had reluctantly gone upstairs, found Dr. Phil's journal. It was filled with sketches of inventions, but the last few pages were different. They detailed strange experiments and a mysterious group known as "The Order of Shadows."

She ran downstairs, journal in hand. "Guys, you have to see this," she said breathlessly. "Dr. Phil was onto something big, and I think it got him into trouble."

As they pieced together the clues, they realized they needed help. But who could they trust? Their parents would never believe them, and the police might think it was just a prank.

Suddenly, Derek had an idea. "What about Mr. Thompson, the retired detective who lives down the street? He always said he was looking for one last big case. Maybe he can help us."

"Let's Go"

CHAPTER III

The Mysterious Mr. Thompson

Mr. Thompson's house was a large, Victorian-style building that seemed to loom over the street. Its dark exterior and overgrown garden gave it a haunted look, especially at night. The triplets hesitated at the gate, their earlier bravado waning. But they knew they had to press on.

Derek took the lead, pushing open the creaky gate. "Come on, guys," he said with a confidence he did not feel. They walked up the cobblestone path and reached the front door. Evan knocked, his knuckles rapping loudly in the silence.

After what felt like an eternity, the door creaked open. Mr. Thompson stood there, a tall, imposing figure with sharp eyes that seemed to pierce through them. He looked at the triplets, his expression unreadable. "What brings you kids here at this hour?" he asked in a gravelly voice.

Alyssa stepped forward, clutching Dr. Phil's journal tightly. "Mr. Thompson, we need your help. Our friend Dr. Phil has been kidnapped, and we found some clues that led us to you."

Mr. Thompson raised an eyebrow. "Kidnapped, you say? Come in, then. Let's hear your story." He stepped aside, allowing them into his dimly lit house.

The interior was just as imposing as the exterior, with dark wood paneling, heavy drapes, and shelves lined with books and odd trinkets. They followed Mr. Thompson into his study, where a large desk covered in papers and strange artifacts dominated the room.

"Sit," Mr. Thompson instructed, gesturing to a worn leather sofa. The triplets sat down, feeling small in the presence of the retired detective.

Derek began explaining everything from the noises Alyssa heard to the clues they found in Dr. Phil's house. Mr. Thompson listened intently, occasionally nodding but saying nothing.

When they finished, he leaned back in his chair, his fingers steepled. "This is quite the tale," he said slowly. "And these clues you found are intriguing. The map, the note, and the journal... they all point to something bigger."

He stood up and began pacing. "The Order of Shadows," he muttered. "I thought they were just a myth, a story told to scare people. But if Dr. Phil was involved with them, then this is serious."

"Do you know who they are?" Alyssa asked, her voice barely above a whisper.

Mr. Thompson nodded. "They're a secretive group rumored to be involved in all sorts of shady dealings—experimenting with forbidden sciences, hoarding ancient artifacts, and manipulating events from the shadows. If Dr. Phil stumbled upon something they wanted, it would explain his disappearance."

He turned to face them. "You kids have done well to find these clues, but this is no ordinary case. It is dangerous. Are you sure you want to continue?"

Derek, Evan, and Alyssa exchanged glances. They were scared, but their determination was stronger. "We have to find Dr. Phil," Evan said firmly. "He's, our friend."

Mr. Thompson nodded, a small smile playing on his lips. "Very well. We will work together. But we must be careful. The Order is powerful, and they won't hesitate to remove anyone who gets in their way."

He moved to his desk and started organizing the papers. "First, we need to decode this map and find out what the 'secret formula' Dr. Phil mentioned is. It might give us a lead on where he's being held."

Derek pulled out the map, spreading it on the desk. Mr. Thompson examined it closely, his eyes narrowing as he traced the markings. "This is no ordinary map. It is encrypted. We'll need to decipher it."

Alyssa handed him the journal. "Maybe there's something in here that can help."

Mr. Thompson flipped through the journal, stopping at the sketches and notes on the Order. "These symbols... they match the ones on the map. We need to find a pattern."

Hours passed as they worked together, piecing together the clues. Mr. Thompson's knowledge of codes and ciphers proved invaluable. Finally, they cracked the code, revealing a hidden message that pointed to an old, abandoned factory on the outskirts of town.

"This is it," Mr. Thompson said, his eyes gleaming with excitement. "We have our first lead. But we must be cautious. The Order won't take kindly to trespassers."

The triplets felt a mix of fear and excitement. They were about to embark on a dangerous mission to rescue their friend. As they prepared to leave, Mr. Thompson handed each of them a small, sleek device. "These are communication devices. We need to always stay in contact. If anything goes wrong, press the panic button."

With a final nod, they set out into the night, determined to uncover the secrets of the Order of Shadows and rescue Dr. Phil.

As they approached the factory, they could not shake the feeling that they were being watched. The shadows seemed to move, and every creak and rustle made them jump. They knew they were walking into a trap, but they had no choice. Their friend's life depended on it.

CHAPTER IV

Into The Shadows

The triplets and Mr. Thompson stood outside the abandoned factory; its towering structure outlined against the night sky. The air was heavy with tension and the faint smell of rust and decay. Derek, Evan, and Alyssa exchanged anxious glances, their hearts racing in their chests.

Mr. Thompson signaled for them to follow him, his resolve unwavering. "Stay close and stay quiet," he whispered, leading the way around the building to a side entrance. The door was ancient and rusty, but surprisingly, it was unlocked. He pushed it open slowly, the hinges squeaking loudly in the silence.

Inside, the factory was a maze of dark, narrow passages and vast, open spaces filled with old machinery and stacks of forgotten boxes. The dim light from their flashlights cast eerie shadows on the walls, making the place feel even more menacing.

As they ventured deeper into the factory, they kept their eyes and ears open for any sign of Dr. Phil or his kidnappers. They were about to turn a corner when they heard a faint sound—a muffled cry for help. Alyssa's heart skipped a beat. "That's him," she whispered urgently. "It has to be Dr. Phil."

Mr. Thompson nodded, motioning for them to follow the sound. They moved cautiously; their steps barely audible on the dusty floor. The cries grew louder as they approached a large room at the end of the hallway. Peeking through a crack in the door, they saw Dr. Phil tied to a chair in the center of the room, surrounded by shadowy figures.

The leader of the group, a tall man with a menacing look, was holding a syringe filled with a glowing liquid—the same fluid Derek had found in the hidden compartment. "Tell us the formula, Dr. Phil, or we'll have to use more... persuasive methods," the leader threatened, his voice cold and cruel.

Dr. Phil, despite his predicament, looked defiant. "I will never tell you, "He spat. "You'll never get your hands on my work."

Mr. Thompson turned to the triplets; his expression grim. "We need to create a distraction and get Dr. Phil out of here." Derek and Evan nodded, slipping away to find something that could make a loud enough noise to draw the captors away. They found a stack of old metal pipes and carefully positioned them near a ledge. With a final nod to each other, they pushed the pipes over the edge, creating a deafening crash.

The shadowy figures in the room jumped, turning their attention towards the sound. "Go check it out," the leader ordered his men. As the captors rushed to investigate, Mr. Thompson and Alyssa slipped into the room.

They hurried to Dr. Phil's side, working quickly to untie him. "We're here to rescue you," Alyssa murmured, her hands trembling with urgency.

Dr. Phil's eyes widened in relief. "Thank you," he said hoarsely. "But we need to hurry. They'll be back any moment."

Just as they freed Dr. Phil, the leader realized the distraction was a ruse. "It's a trap!" he yelled, rushing back into the room. He lunged at Alyssa, but Mr. Thompson intercepted him as the triplets helped Dr. Phil to his feet.

"Run!" Mr. Thompson shouted, holding the leader at bay. "Get out of here!"

The triplets and Dr. Phil dashed out of the room, navigating the labyrinthine hallways of the factory. They could hear pursuit behind them, the footsteps of the gang echoing through the halls. Panic set in as they realized they were being chased.

Derek spotted a narrow passage leading to an emergency exit. "This way!" he called, leading the group down the corridor. They burst through the emergency exit, emerging into the cool night air. They did not stop running until they were far away from the factory, hidden in the shadows of a nearby grove of trees.

Breathing heavily, they collapsed to the ground, their hearts racing. Dr. Phil looked at them with gratitude and concern. "Thank you for saving me," he said, his voice shaky. "But we're not safe yet. The Order won't stop until they get what they want."

Alyssa's resolve shone in her eyes as she nodded. "Dr. Phil, we've got your back. The Order of Shadows doesn't stand a chance against us."

CHAPTER V

Unmasking The Shadows

The woods of trees gave transitory haven, but the triplets and Dr. Phil knew they could not remain covered up for long. Mr Thompson, who had overseen to elude the production line after them, rejoined the bunch, his dress marginally dishevelled but his soul undeterred.

"We require an arrangement," Mr. Thompson said, his voice relentless. "The Arrange won't halt until they have what they need. We require to go on the offensive."

Dr. Phil gestured, his expression grave. "They need my equation. It is an effective vitality source that seems revolutionize the world—or devastate it if utilized disgracefully. We can't let it drop into their hands."

Derek, ever the strategist, talked up. "We require to discover out more almost the Arrange. Who are they? What are their weaknesses?"

Evan proposed, "Possibly we can discover more data in Dr. Phil's lab. There seems to be something we missed, something that can offer assistance to us."

Alyssa, feeling a blend of fear and energy, included, "We too require figuring out who in town we can believe. We can't do this alone."

Mr. Thompson concurred. "We'll part up. Derek and Evan, come with me to check out Dr. Phil's lab. Alyssa, you, and Dr. Phil go back domestic and attempt to accumulate more data from his notes. Remain covered up and remain safe.

The gather part up, each combine moving cautiously through the shadows to maintain a strategic distance from discovery. Derek, Evan, and Mr. Thompson made their way to Dr. Phil's lab, a little, cluttered building behind his house. The lab was filled with interesting gadgets and heaps of inquiries about papers.

Derek started sorting through the papers, looking for anything that might provide them with an edge. "Here's something," he said, holding up an archive. "It's a list of names. These are the members of the Order?"

Mr. Thompson took the list and examined it. "We require to cross-reference these names with known partners of the Arrange. This might offer assistance to `us recognize their pioneers and operatives."

Evan, in the interim, was investigating the lab's capacity zone. He found a bolted cabinet and overseen to pry it open with a screwdriver he found adjacent. Interior were a few vials of the gleaming fluid and a note pad labeled "Equation Experiments."

"Look at this," Evan called, bringing the scratch pad to Derek and Mr. Thompson. "These are point by point notes on the equation. Possibly we can utilize this to figure out how to check it."

While they assembled proof, Alyssa and Dr. Phil made their way back to Dr. Phil's house. They slipped interior discreetly and headed straight for his consider. Dr. Phil pulled out a few covered up records, his hands shaking marginally. "These contain everything I know around the Arrange," he clarified. "Their history, their objectives, their weaknesses."

Alyssa filtered through the records, her eyes broadening as she perused. "This is mind blowing," she said. "They've been around for centuries, controlling occasions and gathering control. But it too says they have a key shortcoming: they depend intensely on central administration. If we can disturb their command structure, we can debilitate them."

Dr. Phil gestured. "Precisely. And we require to act quick some time recently they regroup and come after us again."

As they pored over the reports, they heard a commotion exterior. Alyssa looked through the window ornaments and saw a gathering of shadowy figures drawing closer to the house. "They've found us," she whispered, her heart hustling. "We require to go, now!"

Grabbing the most imperative records, Alyssa and Dr. Phil slipped out the back entryway and ran to meet up with the others at a prearranged secure house—a little, deserted cabin on the edge of town that Mr. Thompson had arranged for emergencies.

Reunited, the bunch rapidly shared what they had found. "We have the names of their individuals, their shortcomings, and notes on the equation," Derek summarized. "But we require a concrete arrange to take them down."

Mr. Thompson gestured, his expression unflinching. "We'll utilize the data we've accumulated to recognize their pioneers and disturb their operations. We'll uncover their insider facts and turn their claim strategies against them."

Dr. Phil included, "And we'll require to discover a way to neutralize the equation so they can't utilize it as a weapon."

The triplets felt a surge of assurance. They had come this distant, and they were not to allow up. Together, they started defining an arrangement, utilizing their combined information and aptitudes to plan for the last standoff with the Arrange of Shadows.

As the night wore on, they knew they were up against an impressive adversary. But with boldness, insights, and the quality of their fellowship, they were prepared to confront anything that lay ahead. The shadows were closing in, but they were prepared to bring the light

CHAPTER VI

Cracking The Code

The safe house was small and cluttered, but it provided the cover they needed. As dawn broke, the triplets, Dr. Phil, and Mr. Thompson sat around a makeshift table, their faces illuminated by the soft light of a single lamp. The air was thick with tension and determination.

"We need to identify the leaders of the Order and find their headquarters," Mr. Thompson said, spreading the documents and notes they had gathered across the table. "Once we have that information, we can plan our next move."

Alyssa scanned the list of names Derek had found. "These people could be anywhere," she said. "How do we figure out who's who?"

Dr. Phil tapped his chin thoughtfully. "We need to cross-reference these names with known public figures and business leaders. The Order often hides in plain sight, using their influence to stay undetected."

Derek, ever the tech-savvy one, pulled out his laptop. "I can run these names through various databases and see what comes up," he said. "It might take some time, but it's our best shot."

As Derek worked on his laptop, Evan flipped through the notebook labeled "Formula Experiments." He frowned at the complex chemical equations and technical jargon. "This is all way over my head," he admitted. "We need someone who understands this stuff."

Dr. Phil took the notebook from Evan and began examining the notes. "I can decipher most of this," he said.

"The formula is based on a rare energy source that amplifies natural abilities. If the Order figures out how to weaponize it, we're in serious trouble."

Alyssa's eyes widened. "We have to stop them," she said firmly. "We need to find a way to neutralize the formula."

Dr. Phil nodded. "I have an idea, but it's risky. There is a counteragent that can neutralize the formula's effects, but it's incredibly volatile. We'll need to synthesize it carefully."

Mr. Thompson leaned forward. "First, we need to secure the lab. If we can set up a secure location to work, we can start synthesizing the counteragent and planning our attack on the Order."

Derek looked up from his laptop, a triumphant smile on his face. "I found something," he said. "Several of the names on the list are linked to a corporation called ShadowTech Industries. It's a front for the Order."

Alyssa's eyes lit up. "That's it," she said. "If we can infiltrate ShadowTech, we can find out where the Order's headquarters are and who their leaders are."

Mr. Thompson nodded. "We'll need to be careful. ShadowTech will have tight security, and the Order won't hesitate to eliminate any threats."

The group quickly formulated a plan. Derek would hack into ShadowTech's systems to gather information, while Mr. Thompson and Evan scouted the building for entry points. Alyssa and Dr. Phil would prepare the lab and start synthesizing the counter-agent.

As the day progressed, they worked tirelessly, each focused on their task. Derek set up his laptop and began hacking into ShadowTech's network, his fingers flying across the keyboard. Evan and Mr. Thompson studied the blueprints of the building, identifying potential entry points and security measures.

In the lab, Dr. Phil and Alyssa worked side by side, carefully measuring and mixing chemicals to create the counter-agent. The process was slow and meticulous, but they could not afford any mistakes.

By nightfall, they had made considerable progress. Derek had successfully infiltrated ShadowTech's network and identified several key figures linked to the Order. "I've got names, addresses, and meeting schedules," he reported. "We can start tracking them down."

Evan and Mr. Thompson had identified a weak point in ShadowTech's security—a rarely used service entrance that could provide covert access to the building. "It's not heavily guarded," Mr. Thompson said. "We can get in and out without attracting too much attention."

Dr. Phil and Alyssa had synthesized a small batch of the counter-agent. "It's not much, but it's a start," Dr. Phil said. "We need to test it to make sure it works."

The group gathered around the table, reviewing their plans, and preparing for the next phase of their mission. They knew the risks were high, but they were determined to see it through.

"We're close," Mr. Thompson said, his voice filled with determination. "We'll take down the Order and save our town. But we need to stay vigilant and work together."

CHAPTER VII

The Infiltration

The night was calm and quiet, a stark contrast to the tension building within the group as they prepared for their infiltration of ShadowTech Industries. The triplets, Dr. Phil, and Mr. Thompson gathered their equipment and reviewed the plan one last time.

"Remember," Mr. Thompson said, his voice low and serious. "Our primary objective is to gather information on the Order's leaders and locate their headquarters. Stay focused and stay safe."

Derek, armed with his laptop and various hacking tools, nodded. "I'll access their internal network and download any relevant data. We'll need to be quick."

Evan checked the small, portable devices they had prepared. "These are miniature cameras and microphones. We'll plant them in key locations to gather intel."

Aylssa, her determination unwavering, looked at Dr. Phil. "Are you ready to evaluate the counter-agent if we find any of the formula?"

Dr. Phil nodded, holding a small vial of the counter-agent they had synthesized. "We need to be sure it works. If we get the chance, we'll assess it on a sample of the formula."

With their plan set, the group made their way to ShadowTech Industries. The building was a modern, glass-and-steel structure, imposing and heavily guarded. They approached the service entrance, the weak point in the security that Mr. Thompson and Evan had identified.

Mr. Thompson used a small device to disable the security cameras temporarily. "We have a five-minute window," he said. "Let's move."

They slipped inside, their movements silent and precise. The interior of the building was a stark contrast to its exterior—sterile, with bright fluorescent lighting and gleaming surfaces. They moved quickly, avoiding the occasional security patrols, and heading for the central server room.

Derek found an access terminal and connected his laptop, working swiftly to break the internal network. "I'm in," he whispered, his fingers flying over the keyboard. "Downloading data now."

Meanwhile, Evan and Mr. Thompson planted miniature cameras and microphones in strategic locations, ensuring they would capture any important conversations or meetings. Aylssa and Dr. Phil kept watch, ready to act if needed.

As Derek continued his download, the tension in the air grew thicker. Suddenly, a security alert flashed on his screen. "We've been detected," he said urgently. "We need to go, now!"

They quickly gathered their equipment and made their way to the exit, but their path was blocked by a group of armed guards. "Stop right there!" one of the guards barked, raising his weapon.

Mr. Thompson stepped forward; his hands raised. "We don't want any trouble," he said calmly. "We're just leaving."

The guard narrowed his eyes. "You're trespassing on private property. You're coming with us."

Derek glanced around, looking for an escape route. "There's a ventilation shaft behind us," he whispered to

Evan. "If we can create a distraction..."

Evan nodded, pulling out a small smoke bomb from his bag. "Cover your eyes," he whispered back, then threw the smoke bomb at the guards' feet.

The room filled with thick, choking smoke, and the guards shouted in confusion. The triplets, Dr. Phil, and Mr. Thompson used the opportunity to slip into the ventilation shaft, crawling through the narrow space until they reached an exit on the other side of the building.

They emerged into a dark alley, gasping for air and adrenaline still pumping. "That was too close," Aylssa said, her heart racing.

Derek held up a USB drive. "But we got the data. Let's get back to the safe house and see what we found."

Back at the safe house, they quickly downloaded and analyzed the data. The files contained detailed information about the Order of Shadows—names, locations, and plans. They also found blueprints for a secret underground facility, the Order's headquarters.

"This is it," Mr. Thompson said, his eyes gleaming with determination. "We've found their base of operations. Now we just need to figure out how to get inside."

Dr. Phil examined the files related to the formula. "And we need to test the counter-agent. If we can neutralize the formula, it will be a huge blow to the Order."

The triplets looked at each other, their determination renewed. They had come so far and faced so many dangers, but the end was finally in sight. They knew the risks were high, but they were ready to take them.

"We'll need to plan our next move carefully," Derek said. "We have the element of surprise, but we can't afford any mistakes."

Mr. Thompson nodded. "We'll study these files and come up with a plan. The Order of Shadows has been a menace for too long. It's time to bring them down."

CHAPTER VIII

The Discovery

Back at the safe house, the group gathered around Derek' laptop, their faces illuminated by the screen's glow. The data they had retrieved from ShadowTech's servers was extensive, but time was of the essence.

"Start with the key names and addresses," Mr. Thompson suggested, leaning over Derek' shoulder. "We need to pinpoint their leaders and headquarters."

Derek nodded, his fingers flying over the keyboard. "I'm on it," he replied, sorting through the files, and cross-referencing them with known public figures and business leaders. "Here's something: several of the names are linked to a private estate on the outskirts of town. It's owned by someone named Aaron Whitewood."

Dr. Phil's eyes widened. "Aaron Whitewood," he muttered. "I've heard that name before. He's a notorious figure in the scientific community, known for his unethical experiments and connections to shady organizations."

Evan glanced at the screen. "So, he's, our guy. We need to find out what's going on at that estate."

Mr. Thompson nodded. "We'll need to surveil the estate and gather as much intel as we can before we make a move."

Aylssa, who had been reading Dr. Phil's notes on the formula, looked up. "I found something important," she said. "According to these notes, Whitewood has been trying to replicate the formula but hasn't succeeded yet. He's missing a crucial component."

Dr. Phil leaned in, examining the notes. "Yes, that's right," he confirmed. "The energy source required for the formula is incredibly rare. If Whitewood gets his hands on it, he'll have everything he needs to complete the formula."

Derek frowned. "We need to find that energy source before he does," he said. "If we can secure it, we can prevent him from finishing the formula and gaining the power he seeks."

Mr. Thompson agreed. "First, we need to gather more information on Whitewood's estate. We'll split into two teams: one to surveil the estate and the other to locate and secure the energy source."

The group quickly formulated their plan. Derek and Evan would manage the surveillance, using their tech skills to monitor Whitewood's activities and identify potential entry points. Aylssa and Dr. Phil would locate the energy source, using Dr. Phil's scientific knowledge and Aylssa's resourcefulness.

As night fell, Derek and Evan set up their equipment near Whitewood's estate. Hidden in a wooded area overlooking the estate, they used high-powered binoculars and a laptop to monitor the property.

"Look," Derek whispered, pointing to a group of people entering the estate. "Those are some of the names from the list. It looks like they're having a meeting."

Evan adjusted the focus on the binoculars. "We need to find out what they're planning," he said. "If we can intercept their communications, we might get a lead on the energy source."

Meanwhile, Aylssa and Dr. Phil were at the safe house, poring over maps and scientific journals. "The energy source we're looking for is called Tritium X," Dr. Phil explained. "It's an incredibly rare element found only in certain remote locations."

Aylssa traced a route on the map. "According to this, there's a location about fifty miles from here where Tritium X was discovered," she said. "It's a long shot, but it's our best chance."

Dr. Phil nodded. "We'll need to move quickly," he said. "If Whitewood's men are also looking for it, we have to get there first."

As the night wore on, Derek and Evan continued their surveillance. They managed to intercept a communication revealing that Whitewood was indeed searching for Tritium X and had sent a team to secure it.

"We need to warn Aylssa and Dr. Phil," Derek said urgently, packing up their equipment. "They're heading straight into danger."

Back at the safe house, Aylssa and Dr. Phil prepared to set out for the remote location. Just as they were about to leave, Derek and Evan burst in, out of breath.

" Whitewood's men are already on their way," Derek warned. "We need to move now and stay one step ahead of them."

"Hmm"

CHAPTER IX

The Race for Tritium X

The triplets, Dr. Phil, and Mr. Thompson set off on their mission, the urgency of their task propelling them forward. The road to the remote location where Tritium X was last discovered was rough and winding, taking them through dense forests and rugged terrain.

Derek drove, his eyes focused on the uneven path ahead. "We need to get there before Whitewood's men," he said, his voice tense. "Every second counts."

Evan, seated in the back, was busy checking their equipment. "We have everything we need," he said, looking up. "But we need to be prepared for anything. Whitewood's men won't give up easily."

Aylssa, sitting next to Evan, reviewed the map again. "According to this, we should be close," she said. "There's a clearing up ahead where the Tritium X was found."

Dr. Phil, riding a shotgun, turned to Derek. "Once we find the Tritium X, we need to secure it and test the counter-agent. It's our only chance to stop Whitewood."

As they approached the clearing, they saw the faint glow of headlights in the distance. "Looks like we're not alone," Mr. Thompson said, his eyes narrowing. "We need to move fast."

They parked the car a short distance away and proceeded on foot, staying low and moving quickly. The clearing was just ahead, and they could see the outlines of Whitewood's men setting up a perimeter around a small cave entrance.

"That must be the place," Aylssa whispered. "We need a distraction."

Evan pulled out a small device from his backpack. "I've got this," he said, grinning. "A little homemade gadget to create a distraction."

He activated the device, and within moments, a loud explosion echoed through the forest, causing Whitewood's men to scatter in confusion. "Go, now!" Evan urged.

The group sprinted towards the cave entrance, slipping past the disoriented guards. Inside, the cave was dark and damp, but the faint glow of Tritium X crystals illuminated their path.

"There it is," Dr. Phil said, pointing to a cluster of glowing crystals embedded in the cave wall. "We need to extract it carefully."

Derek and Evan worked quickly, using their tools to carefully remove the crystals. Meanwhile, Aylssa and Mr. Thompson kept watch, aware that the guards outside would soon regroup.

"Got it," Derek said, holding up a crystal. "Let's test the counter-agent."

Dr. Phil took the crystal and the vial of counter-agent, carefully mixing them. The mixture glowed brightly for a moment before dimming. "It works," he said, relief evident in his voice. "This will neutralize Whitewood's formula."

Suddenly, the sound of footsteps echoed through the cave. "We've got company," Mr. Thompson warned. "We need to get out of here."

The group hurried back towards the cave entrance, only to be confronted by Whitewood's men. "There's no escape," one of them sneered, raising his weapon.

Aylssa stepped forward, holding the vial of neutralized formula. "We have what you're looking for," she said boldly.

"But you're not getting it."

A tense standoff ensued, the air thick with anticipation. Just as the guards moved to attack, Mr. Thompson threw another smoke bomb, filling the cave with thick smoke. "Run!" he shouted.

They dashed through the smoke, disorienting the guards and making their way back to the car. Once inside, Derek hit the gas, speeding away from the cave as fast as the rough terrain allowed.

"We did it," Aylssa said, catching her breath. "We have the Tritium X and the counter-agent."

Dr. Phil nodded, a determined look on his face. "Now we need to get back and stop Whitewood for good."

CHAPTER X

The Final Countdown

The journey back to the safe house was filled with a mix of relief and anxiety. The triplets, Dr. Phil, and Mr. Thompson knew they had struck a significant blow against Whitewood, but the fight was far from over. They needed to act quickly to prevent the Order of Shadows from launching their sinister plan.

As they arrived at the safe house, they were greeted by the familiar, comforting sight of their base of operations. Derek quickly set up his laptop, ready to analyze the data they had gathered.

"We need to find the exact location of their headquarters," Derek said, his fingers flying over the keyboard. "If we can disrupt their operations there, we can put an end to this once and for all."

Evan nodded, unpacking their equipment. "I'll start preparing our gear. We need to be ready for anything."

Aylssa, who had been unusually quiet since their encounter with Whitewood's men, looked at Dr. Phil. "What if we don't make it in time?" she asked, her voice tinged with worry.

Dr. Phil placed a reassuring hand on her shoulder. "We will," he said firmly. "We've come too far to fail now."

Mr. Thompson gathered everyone around the table. "Let's go over the plan," he said. "We have the counter-agent and the Tritium X. Our goal is to infiltrate their headquarters, neutralize the formula, and take down Whitewood."

Derek pulled up a map on his laptop. "According to the data we retrieved, their headquarters is located in an abandoned factory on the outskirts of town," he explained. "It's heavily guarded, but there's a service entrance that we can use to get inside."

Evan pointed to a blueprint of the factory. "We'll split into two teams. One team will create a diversion, while the other team plants the counter-agent in their lab."

Aylssa looked at the map, her determination returning. "I'll go with Dr. Phil to the lab," she said. "We know the most about the formula."

Derek nodded. "Evan and I will manage the diversion. Mr. Thompson, you'll coordinate from here and keep an eye on the security feeds."

The plan was set. They spent the rest of the day preparing their equipment and going over the details. As night fell, they knew it was time to make their move.

They drove to the abandoned factory, parking a safe distance away. The building loomed ahead, its dark, crumbling facade hiding the sinister activities within. They approached cautiously, using the shadows to their advantage.

Derek and Evan moved to the side of the building, preparing their distraction. They set up a series of small explosive devices around the perimeter, designed to draw the guards' attention.

"Ready?" Evan whispered.

Derek nodded, his heart pounding. "Ready as I'll ever be."

They triggered the explosives, and the night was filled with the sound of distant blasts. As expected, the guards rushed to investigate, leaving the service entrance unguarded.

"Go, go, go," Derek urged, motioning for Aylssa and Dr. Phil to move.

Aylssa and Dr. Phil slipped inside, navigating the dark, narrow corridors of the factory. They moved quickly, following the map Derek had provided.

"Almost there," Dr. Phil whispered, holding up a small vial of the counter-agent.

They reached the lab, a sterile, high-tech room filled with equipment and vials of the dangerous formula. Aylssa quickly identified the main storage unit and began to pour the counter-agent into the mixture.

"Let's hope this works," she muttered, watching as the liquid began to neutralize the formula.

Just then, the door burst open, and a group of Whitewood's men stormed in. "What are you doing?" one of them shouted, raising his weapon.

Dr. Phil stepped forward, trying to shield Aylssa. "It's over," he said. "We've neutralized your formula."

The leader of the group sneered. "You think that's going to stop us? You're too late."

Aylssa, refusing to back down, grabbed another vial of counter-agent. "We'll see about that," she said, her voice steady.

Before the guards could react, the factory was rocked by another series of explosions. Derek and Evan had set off their remaining devices, causing chaos and confusion.

"Now!" Dr. Phil shouted, pulling Aylssa towards the exit.

They ran through the corridors, dodging debris and avoiding the panicked guards. As they reached the service entrance, they were met by Derek and Evan, who were out of breath but unhurt.

"Did you, do it?" Derek asked, his eyes wide.

Aylssa nodded, a triumphant smile on her face. "It's done."

Mr. Thompson's voice crackled over their earpieces. "Good work, team. Get out of there and come back to the safe house."

They made their way back to the car, the factory behind them a smoldering ruin. As they drove away, they knew they had dealt a significant blow to the Order of Shadows.

But they also knew this was not the end. Whitewood and his followers would regroup, and they needed to be ready for whatever came next. The triplets, Dr. Phil, and Mr. Thompson were more determined than ever to protect their town and put an end to the Order's sinister plans.

As they approached the safe house, Aylssa looked at her brothers and their allies. "We're not done yet," she said. "But we're getting closer."

Derek nodded. "We'll stop them. Together."

Dr. Phil smiled, a rare expression of pure confidence. "Yes, we will. This is just the beginning of the end for the Order of Shadows."

CHAPTER XI

Unraveling the Conspiracy

Back at the safe house, the atmosphere was tense yet determined. They had successfully neutralized the Tritium X formula at the factory, but they knew their victory was only temporary. Whitewood and the Order of Shadows would not rest until they were defeated finally.

As they gathered around the table, Derek spread out maps and documents retrieved from the factory. "We found something," he said, pointing to a detailed schematic of a hidden underground facility. "This is where they're manufacturing the enhanced formula."

Aylssa leaned forward, studying the map intently. "They must have moved their operations underground to avoid detection," she noted. "But this gives us a chance to strike back."

Dr. Phil nodded thoughtfully. "If we can infiltrate this facility and disable their equipment, we can cripple their ability to produce the formula," he suggested. "But it won't be easy."

Mr. Thompson adjusted his glasses, scanning through the documents. "According to this, the entrance to the facility is heavily guarded," he warned. "We'll need a solid plan to get inside."

Evan tapped his fingers on the table, thinking. "What if we create a diversion again?" he suggested. "Draw their attention away from the entrance while a small team sneaks in."

Derek nodded in agreement. "We could use the same explosive distraction tactic, but we need to time it perfectly," he said, calculating the logistics in his head.

Aylssa looked up from the documents, her eyes narrowing. "We also need to consider what they're planning next," she said, pointing to a coded message intercepted from Whitewood's communication network. "There is a mention of a 'Phase 2' in their plans."

Dr. Phil's brow furrowed. "We can't afford to underestimate them," he said gravely. "We need to move swiftly."

After hours of planning and preparation, they set out under the cover of darkness towards the hidden facility. Derek and Evan took points again, setting up their distraction with precision timing. Explosions rocked the night, drawing the guards away from the entrance.

Aylssa, Dr. Phil, and Mr. Thompson slipped through the chaos, moving swiftly towards the entrance. They found a concealed maintenance door and quietly made their way inside, into the labyrinthine corridors of the underground facility.

The air was cold and damp, the sound of machinery humming ominously in the background. They moved cautiously, avoiding patrolling guards and security cameras. Aylssa consulted the map, leading the way deeper into the facility.

"We're getting close," she whispered, her voice barely audible over the noise.

They reached a central chamber filled with rows of equipment and vats of the enhanced formula. Dr. Phil examined the setup, searching for a way to disable the production.

"We need to shut down their main power source," he decided, pointing to a control panel nearby.

Mr. Thompson nodded, interfacing with the panel. "I'll hack into their system and initiate a shutdown," he said, fingers flying across the keypad.

Aylssa stood guard, her senses alert for any sign of approaching guards. "Hurry," she urged, glancing at the ticking clock on her wristwatch.

With a final keystroke, Mr. Thompson disabled the power grid, plunging the facility into darkness. Emergency lights flickered on, casting eerie shadows across the room.

"We did it," Dr. Phil said, relief evident in his voice. "Their production is halted."

But their victory was short-lived. Alarms blared through the facility, signaling the discovery of intruders. Guards converged on their location; weapons drawn.

"We need to get out of here," Derek shouted over the chaos, covering their retreat.

They ran through the dark corridors, pursued by relentless guards. Explosions rocked the facility as Derek and Evan set off their remaining explosives, creating more confusion and buying them precious seconds.

As they reached the maintenance door, Aylssa paused, glancing back at the facility. "We've slowed them down," she said, determination in her eyes. "But they won't give up."

Dr. Phil nodded, his expression serious. "We've dealt them a blow," he agreed. "But this isn't over yet."

CHAPTER XII

Final Stand

Back at the safe house, exhaustion mingled with determination on their faces. They had struck another blow against Whitewood's operations, but they knew the final confrontation was inevitable. The Order of Shadows was regrouping, and their next move would be crucial.

"We need to anticipate their next move," Aylssa said, her voice tinged with urgency. "They won't stop until they're defeated."

Dr. Phil nodded in agreement. "We've disrupted their production, but Whitewood is resourceful. We need to prepare for a direct confrontation."

Derek paced the room, his mind racing with possibilities. "We have the counter-agent and the knowledge to neutralize their formula," he said. "But we need a plan to confront Whitewood head-on."

Evan sat down, pulling out a map of the town. "We know their headquarters is here," he pointed, tracing a location near the outskirts. "If we strike now, we might catch them off guard."

Mr. Thompson adjusted his glasses, studying the map. "We should also consider uniting support," he suggested. "We can't face them alone."

Aylssa looked at her brothers and Dr. Phil, determination burning in her eyes. "Let's gather our allies," she said. "We need everyone's help to bring an end to this."

They spent the next hours contacting trusted friends and allies, rallying them to their cause. The townspeople, alarmed by the threat posed by the Order of Shadows, joined forces with them, determined to protect their home.

Under the cover of darkness, they moved towards Whitewood's headquarters, a fortified compound surrounded by high walls and guarded by loyal followers. Derek and Evan took points again, setting up a perimeter to secure their approach.

As they breached the compound, alarms blared, signaling their arrival. Guards swarmed from all directions capturing *all* the gang members, with their weapons gleaming in the moonlight. Aylssa and Dr. Phil led the charge, their determination unwavering as they fought side by side with their allies.

Explosions echoed through the night as they pushed deeper into the compound, confronting Whitewood's inner circle. The battle raged on, each side refusing to back down in the face of overwhelming odds.

Amidst the chaos, Aylssa spotted Whitewood, his sinister smile a chilling reminder of the stakes. "It ends here, Whitewood," she shouted, her voice filled with resolve.

Dr. Phil and Derek fought alongside her; their skills honed through countless battles against the Order of Shadows. Evan provided cover fire, his steady aim keeping the enemy at bay.

With a final surge of determination, they cornered Whitewood, the leader of the Order of Shadows. "You've lost," Dr. Phil said, his voice cutting through the din of battle. "It's over."

Whitewood laughed, defiance in his eyes. "You may have won this battle, but the Order will endure," he taunted, his voice filled with venom.

Aylssa stepped forward, "Not this time," she said, her voice steady. "We've taken everything from you."

In a swift motion, she poured the counter-agent into the main vats, watching as the enhanced formula fizzled and dissipated. The threat of the Order of Shadows was finally neutralized, and the gang members were put to jail.

As dawn broke over the town, they stood victorious amidst the wreckage of Whitewood's compound. The townspeople cheered, grateful for their bravery and determination.

Dr. Phil looked at the triplets, pride shining in his eyes. "You've done it," he said, his voice filled with admiration. "You've saved our town."

Aylssa smiled, a sense of peace settling over her. "We couldn't have done it without each other," she said, glancing at her brothers.

They stood together, united in their victory and resolved to protect their town from any future threats. The Order of Shadows was defeated, but their bond and determination remained stronger than ever.

As they walked back to the safe house, the town's gratitude echoed around them. They had faced their greatest challenge and emerged victorious, proving that courage and unity could overcome even the darkest of shadows.

"Guys, wait…"

"What happened Alyssa?"

"Did we capture Aaron Whitewood?"

"…No, we didn't!"

Aaron Whitewood

CHAPTER XIII

The Return

The town of Crestwood had barely begun to heal from the aftermath of the Order of Shadows that happened 6 months ago when rumors started circulating about a new threat. Whispers in the marketplace and hushed conversations in the salon spoke of a shadowy figure seen stalking the outskirts of town, his presence ominous and foreboding.

The sun dipped low on the horizon, casting long shadows across the quiet town. Alyssa, Derek, and Evan had become local legends after their victory over the Order of Shadows. Life had returned to normal, yet the lingering unease of not capturing Whitewood remained.

In a secluded mansion, Aaron Whitewood watched the sunset through stained glass windows. His face, once hidden in the shadows, now bore a faint smile of satisfaction. The defeat at the hands of the triplets had been a setback, but he thrived on challenges.

Whitewood's mansion was a fortress of secrecy and intrigue, filled with relics of forgotten eras and guarded by loyal followers. He stood tall, a figure of authority and mystery, his gaze fixed on the distant town where his plans had been foiled.

"They celebrate now," Whitewood muttered to himself, his voice low and measured. "But they underestimate the depth of my resolve."

In the dimly lit study, maps and schematics adorned the walls, detailing future, and contingencies. Whitewood paced slowly, a mind sharpened by ambition and vengeance.

"They think it's over," he continued, a flicker of amusement crossing his face. "They have no idea what's coming."

A knock echoed through the mansion, and a trusted advisor entered, bowing respectfully. "Sir, preparations for Phase 2 are underway," the advisor announced, a hint of anticipation in his voice.

Whitewood nodded, a glint of anticipation in his eyes. "Good," he replied calmly. "It's time to show them what true power looks like."

As the town below settled into evening tranquility, Aaron Whitewood's mansion buzzed with activity. Plans were set in motion, gears turning silently towards a future where shadows would once again darken the horizon.

The triplets had dealt a blow, but Aaron was far from defeated. His ambitions stretched beyond the town, reaching towards a darkness only he could perceive.

The night deepened, casting a veil of secrecy over Whitewood's mansion. In the heart of the study, surrounded by flickering candlelight, Whitewood and his inner circle convened. The room echoed with the murmur of voices, discussing strategies that would shake the foundations of the town's newfound peace.

"Our spies have confirmed their movements," one advisor reported, his voice barely above a whisper. "They are vigilant, but they cannot foresee what we have planned."

Whitewood nodded, his eyes gleaming with a mixture of determination and satisfaction. "They underestimate us," he declared, his voice carrying an air of certainty. "We will strike where they least expect it."

Maps unfurled across the polished wooden table, illuminated by the glow of strategically placed candles.

Each mark and notation represented a calculated move, a step closer to unraveling the triplets' defenses.

"They have allies," another advisor cautioned, his brow furrowed in concern. "We must ensure our forces are prepared for any resistance."

Whitewood's gaze swept over the room, commanding attention without uttering a word. His presence alone conveyed a sense of authority that galvanized his followers into action.

"We have prepared for this moment," he stated firmly, his tone brooking no dissent. "Our preparations must be flawless."

Outside the mansion, under the cover of darkness, Whitewood's operatives moved with practiced precision. They were shadows in the night, unseen and unheard as they executed their leader's commands.

Meanwhile, in the safe house across town, Alyssa, Derek, Evan, and Dr. Philosopher huddled over maps of their own. Their faces were etched with determination, each contemplating the weight of their responsibility.

"We anticipated this," Dr. Philosopher murmured, his voice a calming presence amidst the tension. "But we must remain vigilant."

Alyssa traced a route on the map, her finger following the town's outskirts where Whitewood's mansion stood. "We need to know their every move," she insisted, her gaze unwavering.

Derek nodded in agreement, his mind already strategizing their next steps. "We can't afford to be caught off guard," he affirmed, his voice resolute.

Evan scanned the perimeter, his eyes narrowing with focus. "We must strengthen our defenses," he suggested, his voice echoing the urgency of their situation.

In the depths of night, as plans unfolded on both sides, the town lay suspended in an uneasy calm. The clash between light and shadow loomed on the horizon, each faction poised for the inevitable confrontation that would determine the town's fate.

CHAPTER XIV

Shadows Stir

The night air hung heavy with anticipation as Aaron Whitewood's plans unfolded in the darkness. From his secluded mansion, he orchestrated his next move with meticulous precision, a chess expert plotting his strategy.

Deep within the labyrinthine corridors of his mansion, Whitewood's loyalists gathered, their faces masked in shadow. They whispered in hushed tones, discussing the intricacies of Phase 2, their voices tinged with reverence for their leader.

"We must strike swiftly," one advisor urged, his eyes gleaming with fervor. "The town remains vulnerable after their recent victory."

Whitewood nodded, his expression unreadable. "They believe they've won," he mused aloud, his voice carrying a dangerous edge. "But victory is temporary. Power is enduring."

Outside, the town slept, unaware of the looming threat that stirred in the shadows. Whitewood's operatives moved with silent efficiency; their movements cloaked in secrecy as they prepared for the next phase of their agenda.

Meanwhile, in the heart of town, Alyssa, Derek, and Evan sensed a shift in the air. Despite their recent triumph, a lingering unease settled over them like a shroud. They gathered at the safe house, their conversations veering towards the future and the uncertainty it held.

"We can't afford to let our guard down," Alyssa insisted, her voice firm with determination. "Whitewood won't rest until he's avenged his defeat."

Derek nodded in agreement; his brow furrowed in thought. "We need to stay one step ahead," he said, echoing their earlier discussions. "Gathering intelligence is key."

Evan glanced out the window, his eyes scanning the quiet streets below. "We should expand our network of informants," he suggested, a plan forming in his mind. "We need to know what Whitewood is planning.

Dr. Philosopher, their steadfast ally, listened intently to their deliberations. "Knowledge is our greatest weapon," he reminded them, his voice a steady anchor in uncertain times. "We must be vigilant."

As the night deepened, Alyssa, Derek, Evan, and Dr. Philosopher resolved to confront the looming threat head-on. Their bond forged through adversity, they braced themselves for the challenges ahead, knowing that the shadows harbored secrets that could unravel their hard-won peace.

In the quiet of the safe house, amidst flickering candlelight, they prepared for the inevitable clash with Aaron Whitewood and the resurgent Order of Shadows.

The following days blurred into a tense dance of preparation and anticipation. Alyssa took charge of reconnaissance, slipping through the town's alleys and streets with a stealth borne of necessity. She kept to the shadows, gathering tidbits of information from whispers in taverns and quiet exchanges in market squares.

Derek and Evan focused on fortifying their defenses, transforming the safe house into a bastion of resistance. They reinforced windows, set up makeshift alarms, and trained tirelessly with Dr. Philosopher in combat tactics. Every creak of a floorboard, every rustle of leaves outside, sent their hearts racing with the possibility of imminent danger.

Dr. Philosopher, with his vast knowledge of science and strategy, became their guiding light. He spent hours poring over maps and schematics, plotting potential escape routes, and analyzing Whitewood's probable courses of action. His calm demeanor belied the intensity of his determination to protect his young companions and the town they held dear.

Meanwhile, at Whitewood's mansion, the air crackled with tension. Advisors scurried through dimly lit corridors, relaying messages, and receiving orders with military precision. The mansion's grand halls echoed with the click of heels and murmurs of intrigue as Whitewood's plan unfolded like the intricate gears of a timepiece.

"Weakness must be exploited," Whitewood declared one evening, his voice carrying through a clandestine meeting in the opulent dining room. "Their unity is their vulnerability."

His advisors nodded in agreement; their faces etched with grim determination. They knew the stakes were high, the future of their clandestine organization hinged on the success of Phase 2. Failure was not an option.

Outside, under the cloak of darkness, Whitewood's operatives moved with calculated intent. They prowled the outskirts of town, mapping patrol routes and identifying blind spots in the triplets' defenses. Each step brought them closer to their target, their loyalty to Whitewood unwavering and their resolve unshakable.

Back at the safe house, Alyssa returned with news of increased activity among Whitewood's forces. She relayed her findings to Derek, Evan, and Dr. Philosopher, who listened intently, absorbing every detail with a sense of grim determination.

"They're planning something big," Alyssa concluded, her voice low but filled with urgency. "We need to be ready."

Derek clenched his fists, his jaw set in determination. "We can't afford any surprises," he said firmly, echoing Alyssa's concern. "We have to anticipate their every move."

Evan nodded in agreement, his mind already racing with strategies. "We'll need to mobilize our allies," he suggested, his voice tinged with the weight of responsibility. "Strength in numbers."

Dr. Philosopher observed them all with a steady gaze, his mind calculating the odds. "Time is against us," he said quietly, his tone a mixture of caution and resolve. "But we have faced adversity before. Together, we will prevail over the conflict, highlighting the preparations and strategies of both sides as they brace for the impending showdown."

CHAPTER XV

The Dawn of Phase 2

The town of Crestwood lay nestled between rolling hills, its streets quiet under the veil of night. But within the walls of the safe house, a sense of urgency hung heavy in the air. Alyssa, Derek, Evan, and Dr. Philosopher gathered around a weathered table strewn with maps and candlelight, their faces etched with determination.

"We've disrupted their operations, but Whitewood won't stay idle," Alyssa declared, her voice cutting through the room's tension. "We need to anticipate their next move."

Derek traced a finger over the map, his brow furrowed in thought. "Our intel suggests they're gearing up for something big," he said, his tone betraying a hint of concern. "We have to be ready."

Evan nodded in agreement, his eyes narrowing as he scanned the perimeter on the map. "If Phase 2 is anything like what we've seen before, they'll strike hard and fast," he warned, his voice tinged with the weight of experience.

Dr. Philosopher studied the maps and diagrams spread before them, his mind racing with possibilities. "Whitewood is cunning," he remarked, his voice a calm counterpoint to the urgency in the room. "We must prepare for the unexpected."

Outside the safe house, the town slept, unaware of the looming threat that stirred in the shadows. Whitewood's operatives moved with silent purpose; their movements masked by the darkness as they prepared to execute Phase 2 of their sinister plan.

At Whitewood's mansion, a pall of anticipation hung over the dimly lit chambers. Advisors gathered around a table strewn with maps and blueprints, their faces illuminated by the flickering light of oil lamps. Aaron Whitewood stood at the head of the table, his presence commanding respect and obedience.

"The time for subtlety has passed," Whitewood declared, his voice a low rumble that reverberated through the room. "Phase 2 will test our resolve and reveal our strength."

His advisors nodded solemnly, their expressions a mix of determination and apprehension. They understood the gravity of their mission—to strike at the heart of Crestwood's defenses and seize control before dawn broke.

Outside the mansion, Whitewood's operatives prepared for their mission with meticulous precision. They donned masks and dark clothing, their weapons gleaming in the moonlight as they moved in disciplined formation. Their steps were purposeful, their breaths shallow with anticipation of the coming conflict.

Back at the safe house, Alyssa and her brothers reviewed their defenses with a critical eye. They reinforced barricades and set up lookout posts, their movements swift and coordinated. Each action was a testament to their unity and determination to protect their home from the encroaching darkness.

"We need to gather more intel," Alyssa insisted, her voice unwavering. "We can't afford to be caught off guard."

Derek nodded; his jaw set in determination. "Our informants are our eyes and ears," he agreed, his gaze flicking to the window as if expecting trouble to appear at any moment. "We need to push them for every detail."

Evan paced the room, his mind racing with strategy. "If Whitewood strikes, we strike back," he declared, his voice firm and resolute. "We won't let them take us by surprise."

Dr. Philosopher, ever the voice of reason, nodded thoughtfully. "Preparation is our greatest asset," he reminded them, his gaze steady as he met each of their eyes in turn. "We must anticipate their every move and be ready to adapt."

As midnight approached, tension mounted in the safe house. The air crackled with anticipation, each breath laden with the promise of imminent conflict. Outside, the town lay quiet, unaware of the storm gathering on its doorstep.

Inside the safe house, Alyssa, Derek, Evan, and Dr. Philosopher stood united against the gathering darkness. Their resolve was unyielding, their bond forged through adversity and strengthened by their shared determination to protect Crestwood from those who sought to harm it.

The night stretched on, the hours ticking by intense silence. Candlelight flickered over maps and weapons, casting dancing shadows on the walls. Outside, the moon hung low in the sky, its pale light a stark contrast to the shadows that prowled the town's outskirts.

As the first whispers of dawn painted the horizon, the safe house remained a bastion of defiance against the encroaching threat. Alyssa, Derek, Evan, and Dr. Philosopher stood vigilant; their eyes fixed on the horizon as they awaited the inevitable clash that would determine Crestwood's fate.

CHAPTER XVI

Shadows of the Past

The victory at the factory had given Crestwood a brief respite, but the sense of impending danger lingered. Alyssa, Derek, Evan, and Dr. Philosopher gathered at their safe house, the weight of their mission pressing down on them.

Alyssa paced back and forth, her mind racing. "Whitewood will not stop. We need to figure out what he is planning next."

Derek leaned over the map spread out on the table. "We need more information. Our current intel is not enough."

Evan, who usually preferred to listen rather than speak, finally broke his silence. "I know someone who can help. An old friend of Dad's. He might have some useful information about Whitewood."

Alyssa and Derek exchanged curious glances. "Who is it?" Alyssa asked.

Evan took a deep breath. "Captain Reynolds. He served with Dad during the war. If anyone knows Whitewood's history and motives, it is him."

Dr. Philosopher's eyes lit up with interest. "An old comrade from the war. That could be exactly what we need. Where can we find him?"

Evan pointed to a location on the map. "He lives near the old mill on the outskirts of town."

Without hesitation, they set out for the outskirts, the evening sky growing darker as they approached the old mill. The air was thick with tension, each step echoing their determination.

Captain Reynolds cabin was a small, weathered structure surrounded by dense woods. The man himself was a rugged figure, his eyes sharp and wary as he opened the door. "What brings you here?" he asked, his voice rough and guarded.

"We need your help," Alyssa said urgently. "We're up against Aaron Whitewood."

At the mention of Whitewood's name, Reynolds expression hardened. "Whitewood... I never thought I would hear that name again. He was always ambitious and ruthless. Even back then, he had plans that went beyond the war."

Derek leaned forward. "We need to know more about him. Anything that can help us understand his next move."

Reynolds sighed heavily, sinking into an old armchair. "Whitewood was obsessed with power. After the war, he disappeared. We thought he was dead, but clearly, he is back."

Dr. Philosopher's eyes narrowed thoughtfully. "Did he have any allies? People who might still be loyal to him?"

Reynolds nodded slowly. "A few. Men who shared his vision of a new order. They were always talking about creating a utopia, but their methods were extreme."

Evan leaned in, his face earnest. "Do you know where we can find any of them?"

Reynolds rubbed his temples, deep in thought. "There is one name that comes to mind. Liam Gladstone. He was Whitewood's go-to person. If anyone knows Whitewood's plans, it is him."

Alyssa felt a surge of hope. "Where can we find Gladstone?"

Reynolds looked out the window, his gaze distant. "Last I heard, he was hiding in the ruins of the old city, north of here. But be careful. Gladstone is as dangerous as Whitewood."

They thanked Reynolds for his help and left the cabin with renewed purpose. The path ahead was clear—they needed to find Liam Gladstone and uncover Whitewood's plans.

As they traveled back to Crestwood, the setting sun cast long shadows over the landscape. The town seemed peaceful, but Alyssa knew that darkness was never far away. Whitewood's reach was long, and they had to stay vigilant.

Back at the safe house, they gathered around the table again, their resolve strengthened by Reynolds' revelations. The road ahead was perilous, but they were united in their mission.

"We have a lead," Alyssa said, her voice steady. "Liam Gladstone. If we can find him, we can get ahead of Whitewood."

Derek nodded. "We will need to be careful. Gladstone will not be easy to track down, and he's likely to be well-guarded."

Dr. Philosopher adjusted his glasses, a thoughtful expression on his face. "We will need to prepare for anything. But we have an advantage—Whitewood does not know we're coming."

Evan smiled, determination shining in his eyes. "Let's make it count."

As they planned their next move, the weight of their mission settled over them. They were up against a formidable foe, but they had something Whitewood lacked—a bond forged in trust and loyalty.

The journey to the old city would be their next test, a step deeper into the shadows of the past. But they were ready to face whatever lay ahead, determined to protect their home and bring an end to Whitewood's reign of terror.

With their resolve unwavering, they set their sights on the ruins of the old city, where answers...and danger...awaited.

CHAPTER XVII

Into the Ruins

The ancient city lay in ruins, a stark update of a time long past. Its rotting buildings and disintegrating roads talked of overlooked histories and deserted lives. Alyssa, Derek, Evan, and Dr. Logician stood at the edge of the city, the weight of their mission overwhelming on their shoulders.

"Are you sure about this?" Derek asked, glancing at Evan. "Gladstone's dangerous. This place gives me the creeps."

Evan nodded; his face set with determination. "We don't have a choice. If Gladstone knows Whitewood's plans, we have to find him."

Alyssa tightened her grip on her flashlight, peering into the darkened streets. "Stay close and keep quiet. We don't know what—or who—we might run into."

They moved cautiously, their footsteps echoing through the empty alleyways. The air was thick with dust and the faint scent of decay. Every shadow seemed to hide a potential threat; every sound amplified by the eerie silence of the abandoned city.

Dr. Philosopher adjusted his glasses, his eyes scanning the area. "This place is a maze. We need to be careful not to get lost."

Evan pointed to a dilapidated building ahead. "Reynolds said Gladstone was hiding out in one of the old government buildings. That looks like a good place to start."

As they approached the building, a sudden noise made them freeze. Alyssa signaled for silence, her heart pounding in her chest. They waited, listening intently. The noise came again—a faint rustling, followed by a soft thud.

Derek whispered, "It might be rats. Or it might be Gladstone."

They crept forward, their eyes straining in the dim light. The inside of the building was in worse condition than the outside. Papers and debris littered the floor, and the walls were covered in graffiti and grime.

"Over here," Evan whispered, pointing to a staircase. "Let's check upstairs."

They ascended the creaky stairs, each step threatening to give them away. At the top, they found a series of rooms, their doors hanging ajar. One room, however, was different. Its door was closed, and a faint light seeped through the cracks.

Alyssa signaled for the others to follow her lead. She approached the door, her hand trembling slightly as she reached for the handle. She turned it slowly, pushing the door open with a soft creak.

Inside, the room was sparsely furnished—a table, a few chairs, and a makeshift bed. Sitting at the table, scribbling furiously on a piece of paper, was Liam Gladstone. He looked up, startled, as the door opened.

"Who are you?" Gladstone demanded, his eyes narrowing.

Alyssa stepped forward, her voice steady. "We're not your enemies. We're here to stop Aaron Whitewood."

Gladstone's expression hardened. "Whitewood... Why should I trust you?"

Derek stepped forward. "Because we want the same thing. To stop him before he destroys everything."

Gladstone's gaze flicked between them; suspicion etched on his face. "And you think I can help you?"

Dr. Philosopher nodded. "We know you were his right-hand man. You must know something about his plans."

Gladstone sighed, leaning back in his chair. "I thought I could escape this life. But Whitewood's shadow is long. Alright, I will help you. But you need to understand—this won't be easy."

Alyssa felt a surge of relief. "We didn't expect it to be. Just tell us what you know."

Gladstone began to speak, his voice low and filled with regret. "Whitewood has always been obsessed with power and control. His plans are always meticulously crafted. He uses fear and chaos to manipulate those around him. And he is not working alone. There are others—followers who believe in his vision of a new order."

Evan asked, "Do you know where he is now? What his next move might be?"

Gladstone nodded slowly. "He's been setting up bases in various locations, preparing for something big. I do not know all the details, but I know he has a central base in the mountains. It is heavily guarded and fortified. That's where you'll find him."

Derek clenched his fists. "Then that's where we'll go."

Gladstone held up a hand. "Wait. You can't just walk in there. You'll need a plan, and you will need allies. Whitewood's followers are loyal and dangerous."

Dr. Philosopher nodded. "We understand the risks. But we must stop him. We have to protect our town."

Gladstone looked at them, his expression a mix of hope and fear. "Then you'll need this," he said, reaching into a drawer and pulling out a map. "It's a layout of the base. It might give you an edge."

Alyssa took the map, gratitude in her eyes. "Thank you, Gladstone. We won't let you down."

As they left the building, the weight of their mission felt heavier than ever. The path ahead was clear—they needed to find Liam Gladstone and uncover Whitewood's plans.

They returned to Crestwood; their resolve strengthened by Gladstone's information. The final confrontation was drawing near, and they knew they had to be ready.

"We need to prepare," Alyssa said, her voice firm. "Gather our allies, plan our approach. This is our chance to end this."

Derek, Evan, and Dr. Philosopher nodded in agreement. They had faced many challenges, and prepared to bring an end to Whitewood's rule of terror.

CHAPTER XVIII

Secrets in the Shadows

The sun dipped below the horizon, casting long shadows over Crestwood. The town seemed peaceful, but Alyssa, Derek, Evan, and Dr. Philosopher knew better. The intel from Gladstone had given them hope, but also a sense of urgency. Whitewood's plans were advancing, and they needed a strategy.

"We need more information," Alyssa said, breaking the tense silence in the safe house. "We can't just wait for Whitewood to make his move."

Derek nodded. "Gladstone's intel is a start, but we need to know Whitewood's next steps. And we need allies."

Dr. Philosopher leaned back, considering their options. "There's someone who might help. An old contact of mine, Cristina. She's... well, let's just say she has a knack for finding out things people don't want to find out."

"Where do we find her?" Evan asked.

"She operates out of the old railway station. It's risky, but she's our best shot."

With that, they divided their tasks. Alyssa, Derek, and Evan would go to the railway station. Dr. Philosopher would stay back and coordinate with the rest of their allies.

The railway station was a relic of a bygone era, its grandeur faded into decay. As they approached, the eerie silence was punctuated only by the distant hum of the town. Alyssa knocked on a weathered door, and after a tense moment, it creaked open to reveal a woman with sharp eyes and an air of mystery.

"Phil's friends?" she asked, scrutinizing them.

"We need your help, Cristina," Alyssa said.

Cristina ushered them inside, where maps and papers were strewn across a dusty table. "Whitewood's operation is extensive," she began, her voice low. "He's got safe houses, loyal followers, and he's heavily fortified. But there is a weak link: a secondary base in the industrial district. It's less secure."

Derek leaned in. "Can you help us get in?"

"I can give you the details," Cristina said. "But you'll have to do the rest."

As they left the station, their minds were racing with plans. Back at the safe house, they spread out Cristina's notes. Dr. Philosopher joined them, his expression grave.

"This gives us a fighting chance," he said, looking over the intel. "We need to disrupt Whitewood's operations at the secondary base. It's our best shot."

For the next few days, they prepared meticulously. Volunteers from the town trained under Derek and Evan's guidance, while Alyssa coordinated supplies and organization. The air was thick with anticipation.

On the night of the operation, they moved under the cover of darkness. The industrial district, a maze of rusting machinery, provided perfect cover. Derek and Evan led the infiltration team, while Dr. Philosopher and Alyssa set off a series of distractions to draw the guards away.

Inside the base, they worked quickly. Evan photographed documents and maps while Derek kept watch. Alyssa's heart pounded as they gathered as much information as they could.

Just as they were about to leave, footsteps echoed down the hall. They froze. Alyssa signaled for silence, her mind racing.

"We need to move," she whispered.

They slipped out just as the guards returned, making their way back to the safe house with their hearts in their throats. The relief was palpable as they burst through the door.

Dr. Philosopher looked up, his eyes wide with concern. "Did you get it?"

Alyssa nodded, holding up the documents. "We got everything. This is it."

As they pored over the new intel, the enormity of Whitewood's plans became clear. It was more dangerous than they had imagined, but they were ready.

"We know his weak points," Derek said. "Now we need to act."

Dr. Philosopher smiled, a rare glint of hope in his eyes. "We will. And this time, we'll be ready."

CHAPTER XIX

Echoes of the Past

As dawn broke over Crestwood, the air was thick with the tension of the impending confrontation. In the safe house, Alyssa, Derek, Evan, and Dr. Philosopher gathered to review their plans. The room buzzed with a quiet intensity; each person focused on their tasks.

Alyssa spread out the map of the industrial district on the table. "We need to hit them hard and fast," she said. "The longer we stay, the more dangerous it gets."

Derek nodded, his eyes scanning the routes they had marked. "We need to create a distraction big enough to pull the guards away from the base, but not so big that we can't handle it."

Dr. Philosopher, leaning over the map, pointed to a section of the district. "This area is critical. If we can take out their communications here, it will give us a significant advantage."

Evan looked up from his notes. "And we need to secure an escape route. We can't afford to get trapped inside."

They spent the next few hours finalizing their plans, assigning roles, and checking their equipment. The weight of the mission pressed heavily on their shoulders, but their resolve was unwavering.

As the sun set, they moved out, blending into the shadows. The industrial district loomed ahead, its rusting structures and abandoned machinery casting eerie silhouettes in the fading light. Alyssa, Derek, and Evan led the infiltration team, while Dr. Philosopher and a group of volunteers prepared to create the necessary distractions.

The signal came, and the night erupted in chaos. Explosions and smoke filled the air, drawing the guards away from their posts. Alyssa's heart pounded as they moved swiftly, slipping past the distracted guards and into the heart of the base.

Inside, the base was a labyrinth of corridors and rooms, each filled with equipment and documents. They moved quickly, gathering as much information as they could. Evan worked diligently, photographing, and copying everything they found.

Derek kept an eye on the time. "We need to move, now," he whispered urgently. "They'll be back any minute."

As they turned a corner, they stumbled upon a locked door with a heavy padlock. Alyssa's instincts kicked in. "This looks important," she said, gesturing for Evan to pick the lock.

The lock clicked open, and they pushed the door open to reveal a room filled with maps, plans, and a large, ominous-looking device. Alyssa's eyes widened. "This must be Whitewood's main operation control."

They quickly gathered as much information as they could. Derek snapped photos of the maps, while Alyssa studied the device, trying to understand its purpose.

Suddenly, footsteps echoed down the hall. They froze, the tension thick in the air. Alyssa signaled for silence, her mind racing for an escape route. The footsteps grew louder, and the door began to creak open.

Thinking fast, Derek grabbed a nearby crate and threw it through a window, shattering the glass and creating a loud crash. The footsteps halted, then moved quickly towards the noise. They took the chance and slipped out of the room, hearts pounding.

They made their way back through the maze of corridors, avoiding the guards now converging on the broken window. The distraction team had done their job well, creating enough chaos to cover their escape.

Back at the safe house, they collapsed into chairs, adrenaline still coursing through their veins. Dr. Philosopher looked up from his seat, relief washing over his face. "Did you get it?"

Alyssa nodded, holding up the stack of documents and the photographs. "We got everything. This is our chance."

As they reviewed the new intel, a clearer picture of Whitewood's plans emerged. It was more sinister and far-reaching than they had imagined, but they now had the information they needed to stop him.

Derek pointed to a section of the map. "This is where we need to strike next. It's the heart of his operation."

Evan looked up, determination in his eyes. "We need to move fast. Every moment we wait gives Whitewood more time to regroup."

Dr. Philosopher nodded. "We'll gather our forces and prepare for the final assault. This ends now."

CHAPTER XX

Shadows of the Past

The safe house, now bustling with activity, felt like the beating heart of Crestwood's resistance. Every room was filled with townspeople, each person contributing to the effort in their own way. Some were preparing medical supplies, others were sharpening weapons, and a few were deep in strategy discussions.

Alyssa stood at the center of it all, feeling a mix of pride and anxiety. She watched as Derek, Evan, and Dr. Philosopher worked tirelessly; their faces set with determination. Despite their exhaustion, there was a fire in their eyes—a fire that matched her own.

"Alright, everyone, gather around," Alyssa called out, her voice strong and clear. The room quieted as people turned to listen. "We've made quick progress, but Whitewood's main operation is still active. We need to hit them hard and fast. This will be our final push."

Derek, standing beside her, added, "We'll split into three teams. Team A will lead the primary assault. Team B will secure the perimeter and prevent any escapes. Team C will create diversions and provide support."

Evan, who had been studying the map, chimed in. "I'll lead Team B. We'll ensure that no one gets in or out without us knowing. We can't afford any surprises."

Dr. Philosopher, looking over the plans, nodded in agreement. "And remember, Whitewood is cunning. We must be prepared for anything."

As the teams finalized their preparations, the gravity of the situation settled over them. This was it—the culmination of weeks of planning and countless sacrifices. The townspeople were ready, but they knew this would be no easy battle.

Night fell, and the teams moved out, blending into the shadows. The industrial district loomed ahead, its structures dark and foreboding against the night sky. They advanced silently, every step bringing them closer to the showdown.

Team A, led by Derek, was the first to engage. They slipped past the outer defenses, their movements precise and silent. The guards, distracted by Team C's diversions, were caught off guard. Inside the compound, chaos reigned as Whitewood's followers scrambled to respond.

Alyssa led her team through the maze of corridors, each step taken with caution. They encountered resistance, but their training and resolve saw them through. The sounds of battle echoed around them—shouts, gunfire, the clang of metal.

Outside, Evan's team held the perimeter. They intercepted several escape attempts, each skirmishing a test of their resolve and skill. The town's defenders, ordinary people pushed to extraordinary acts, fought with fierce determination.

Dr. Philosopher, monitoring from a secure location, kept the teams coordinated. "Team A, you're approaching the command center. Stay sharp."

Alyssa's heart raced as they neared their target. A heavily fortified door stood in their way. "This is it," she whispered. "We take this, and it's over."

Derek and another team member set charges on the door, the explosion that followed a signal that the final confrontation had begun. They stormed in, weapons ready, to find Whitewood waiting with his most loyal followers.

"You think you've won?" Whitewood sneered. "This is just the beginning."

Alyssa stepped forward, her resolve unshaken. "It ends here, Whitewood."

The room erupted in chaos. Alyssa and Derek fought side by side, their movements synchronized, each covering the other. Whitewood's followers, though skilled, were no match for their determination.

Alyssa's eyes locked onto Whitewood's. She saw the madness, the twisted purpose driving him. "You've caused enough pain," she said. "It's time to stop."

Whitewood lunged, but Alyssa was faster. She sidestepped, delivering a precise blow that disarmed him. "It's over," she said again, her voice filled with finality.

Silence fell as Whitewood was subdued. His followers, seeing their leader defeated, surrendered. The battle was won, but the cost had been high.

Back at the safe house, they regrouped. Dr. Philosopher looked at the exhausted but triumphant faces around him. "We did it," he said softly. "Crestwood is safe, thanks to all of you."

Alyssa, her heart heavy with the weight of their victory, looked out at the town she had fought to protect. "We couldn't have done it without each other," she said. "But we must stay vigilant. This isn't the end."

CHAPTER XXI

Betrayal?

The aftermath of their victory over Whitewood was bittersweet. Crestwood felt relieved, yet within the safe house walls, a sense of unease lingered. Alyssa, Derek, Evan, and Dr. Philosopher gathered around a table strewn with maps and documents, their faces grave with concern.

"We can't ignore the possibility," Alyssa said, her voice cutting through the tense silence. "There's someone feeding information to Whitewood. That's the only way he could have been so prepared."

Derek nodded, his eyes scanning over a list of recent communications intercepted from Whitewood's compound. "These encrypted messages indicate someone on the inside," he said, pointing to a series of coded notes. "We need to find out who."

Evan, leaning forward with a frown, added, "It could be anyone. Someone close to us, someone we trust."

Dr. Philosopher, ever the strategist, interjected, "Let's start with what we know. The messages reveal details of our plans and movements. Whoever it is, they have access to sensitive information."

They spent hours dissecting the intercepted messages, searching for any clue that could lead them to the mole. Alyssa pored over lists of names, trying to discern patterns or connections. Derek meticulously analyzed the encryption patterns, hoping to find a breakthrough.

"We need to think like Whitewood," Alyssa said, frustration evident in her voice. "He's cunning, but he's fallible. There must be a slip-up somewhere."

Evan, always practical, suggested, "What about physical evidence? Something in Whitewood's compound that could point to who he was in contact with."

Dr. Philosopher nodded thoughtfully. "It's worth a shot. We'll return to the compound, search for anything that might give us a lead."

Back at Whitewood's abandoned office, they combed through the remnants of his operation. Files were scattered, computers lay dormant, and the air was thick with the scent of defeat. Alyssa sifted through paperwork, her eyes scanning for names or notes that could incriminate.

"Here," Derek called out, his voice tinged with energy and concern. "I found a record. It records contacts and installments made to different individuals."

Dr. Philosopher joined him, examining the ledger with a critical eye. "These transactions," he murmured, tracing a line with his finger. "Some of them are recent. They could be our mole."

Alyssa studied the ledger, recognizing names of trusted associates and town officials. "This can't be right," she muttered, disbelief coloring her tone. "These are people we've worked with for years."

Evan, scanning the room for any hidden compartments or clues, added, "Whitewood was thorough. He covered his tracks well, but there must be something we're missing."

As they continued their search, Alyssa stumbled upon a locked drawer. "This could be it," she said, pulling out a set of keys found nearby. With trembling hands, she unlocked the drawer, revealing a hidden compartment filled with encrypted USB drives.

Derek took one of the drives, inserting it into a nearby computer. "Let's see what's on here," he said, his fingers dancing over the keyboard as he worked to decrypt the files.

Hours passed as they uncovered piece after piece of the puzzle. The files contained detailed communications between Whitewood and an unknown contact, discussing plans, strategies, and vulnerabilities within Crestwood's defenses.

"There," Derek said finally, pointing to a decrypted message. "It's from our mole."

They read the message, its contents confirming their worst fears. The mole had been feeding Whitewood information for months, betraying their trust and endangering everyone they cared about.

"These changes everything," Dr. Philosopher said quietly, his voice heavy with disappointment. "We have to confront them."

Alyssa's heart sank as she realized the depth of the betrayal. "But who could it be?"

CHAPTER XXII

The Cat's out of the Bag

The revelation of the mole cast a long shadow over Crestwood. The safe house, once a hub of strategy and camaraderie, now simmered with suspicion and tension. Alyssa, Derek, Evan, and Dr. Philosopher gathered around a dimly lit table, their faces reflecting the gravity of their situation.

"We can't afford to trust anyone blindly now," Derek muttered, his eyes fixed on the floor as if searching for answers there.

Alyssa nodded; her brow furrowed with determination. "We need to root out the mole before they can do any more damage. But how do we do that without tipping our hand?"

Evan leaned forward; his hands clenched into fists. "We can start by narrowing down our suspects. It must be someone who had access to our plans and knew our movements."

Dr. Philosopher interjected, "And someone who had reason to collaborate with Whitewood. We need to think strategically about who could benefit from betraying us."

They spent hours dissecting the decrypted messages and combing through the ledger. Each name on the list of contacts was scrutinized, every interaction analyzed for potential motives.

"It could be anyone," Alyssa said, frustration lacing her voice. "But we must find out. Lives are at stake."

Derek tapped his fingers on the table, lost in thought. "What if we set a trap? Feed false information to our suspects and see who takes the bait."

Dr. Philosopher nodded thoughtfully. "It's risky, but it might be our best chance. We'll need to be careful not to reveal our hand too soon."

They formulated a plan, each step calculated to draw out the mole without alerting them to their suspicions. They would pretend to prepare for an assault on a decoy target, watching closely for any suspicious behavior or communication.

Days passed in tense anticipation. They maintained a facade of normalcy, all the while watching and waiting for a slip-up. The atmosphere in the safe house was thick with paranoia, trust strained to its breaking point.

Then, a breakthrough came unexpectedly. One of the suspects, a town official known for their meticulous mindfulness, showed signs of agitation during a routine meeting. They seemed overly interested in the organization of the decoy operation, asking probing questions that raised eyebrows.

"It's them," Evan said quietly, his eyes meeting Alyssa's with grim certainty. "They're the mole."

Alyssa felt a mix of anger and sadness. This person had been a trusted ally, someone they had relied on in times of crisis. Now, their betrayal threatened everything for which they had fought.

"We confront them tonight," she decided, her voice steady despite the turmoil inside. "We can't afford to wait any longer."

That evening, they gathered in a secluded room, the suspect brought in under the guise of discussing strategy. The tension was palpable as accusations hung in the air.

"You've been working with Whitewood," Derek said, his voice cold and accusing. "Feeding him information about our plans."

The suspect's eyes darted nervously, their facade crumbling under the weight of the evidence against them. "I... I had no choice," they stammered, desperation creeping into their voices. "He threatened my family. I had to protect them."

Dr. Philosopher shook his head, disappointment etched on his face. "There's always a choice," he said firmly. *"And you chose to betray us."*

CHAPTER XXIII

Reckoning

With the mole exposed and Crestwood reeling from betrayal, tensions simmered beneath the surface like a storm waiting to break. Alyssa, Derek, Evan, and Dr. Philosopher gathered once more in the safe house, their minds racing with the weight of recent events.

"We can't let our guard down," Alyssa said, her voice firm with resolve. "There may be others out there, waiting to exploit our vulnerabilities."

Derek nodded in agreement; his jaw set with determination. "We need to strengthen our defenses, both physical and strategic. We can't afford another breach."

Dr. Philosopher, pacing the room with a furrowed brow, added, "And we must rebuild trust among our allies. This betrayal has shaken us to the core."

They spent days fortifying the safe house, tightening security measures, and reviewing protocols. Each member of their team underwent rigorous scrutiny, their loyalty evaluated in the crucible of suspicion.

"We need to get back on the offensive," Evan suggested one evening, breaking the tense silence that had settled over them. "Whitewood may be gone, but his legacy lives on. We must root out his remaining followers."

Alyssa nodded, her mind already racing with plans. "We start by gathering intelligence. We need to know who's still loyal to his cause."

They reached out to informants and allies, cautiously probing for any signs of lingering loyalty to Whitewood. It was slow and painstaking work, but their determination never wavered.

Then, a breakthrough came unexpectedly. An informant tipped them off about a hidden cache of weapons and supplies, rumored to be stashed in an abandoned warehouse on the outskirts of town.

"We need to investigate," Derek said, his eyes alight with renewed purpose. "If Whitewood's followers are still operating, we can't afford to ignore this."

Under cover of darkness, they approached the warehouse, senses on high alert. The air was thick with anticipation as they cautiously entered, scanning the shadows for any sign of movement.

Inside, they found crates of weapons, ammunition, and supplies meticulously organized. It was clear that someone had been planning for a resurgence, preparing for a future conflict.

"These changes everything," Dr. Philosopher murmured, his voice barely audibles over the sound of their collective realization. "Whitewood's network is more entrenched than we thought."

They seized the cache, gathering evidence that would expose the extent of Whitewood's influence even after his defeat. Each item they cataloged was a testament to their ongoing struggle, a reminder that their fight was far from over.

As they returned to the safe house, the weight of their discovery hung heavy in the air. They knew they had to act swiftly, but they also needed to tread carefully. The stakes were higher than ever, and the consequences of failure could be devastating.

"We'll dismantle this network, piece by piece," Alyssa declared, her voice ringing with conviction. "We owe it to Crestwood to *finish* what *we* started."

CHAPTER XXIV

Unmasking the Betrayer

The revelation of the hidden cache sent ripples of tension through Crestwood. Alyssa, Derek, Evan, and Dr. Philosopher knew their battle was far from over. With every step forward, the echoes of Whitewood's legacy pulled them two steps back. But they were resolute—this was a fight they couldn't afford to lose.

Back at the safe house, the atmosphere was charged with a renewed sense of urgency. Maps and blueprints covered the walls, and the hum of strategic discussions filled the air. They knew they had to dismantle Whitewood's network completely, or risk facing the same dangers again.

"We need to trace these supplies back to their source," Alyssa stated, her eyes sharp with determination. "If we can cut off their resources, we can cripple their operations."

Evan, always the pragmatist, suggested, "We should also look into the financial records we found. There might be a paper trail that leads us to their financiers."

Dr. Philosopher nodded thoughtfully. "Agreed. But we must be cautious. Whoever is funding this has a personal stake in keeping their identity hidden. They'll be dangerous."

Their investigation took them deep into the underbelly of Crestwood, following a labyrinthine trail of shell companies and anonymous donors. Each step brought them closer to understanding the scope of Whitewood's influence, but also deeper into a web of deceit and danger.

One night, while sifting through a particularly dense stack of financial records, Derek stumbled upon a name that sent chills down his spine. "Look at this," he said, handing the document to Alyssa. "It's a transaction from an account linked to someone we know."

Alyssa's eyes widened as she read the name. "This can't be right," she whispered, disbelief mingling with a growing sense of dread. "This account belongs to Mr. Thompson."

"WHAT!"

Evan's face hardened. "We trusted him. He was one of our closest allies."

Dr. Philosopher's expression was grim. "We need to confront him, but we must do it carefully. If he's involved, he won't hesitate to protect himself."

The next day, they arranged a meeting with Mr. Thompson under the guise of seeking his advice on their ongoing operations. The air was thick with tension as they approached his home, each of them prepared for the possibility of betrayal.

Mr. Thompson greeted them warmly, his demeanor as affable as ever. But beneath the surface, Alyssa could sense a guardedness, a wariness that hadn't been there before.

"We need to talk," Derek began, his voice steady but filled with an underlying tension. "We found some financial records linked to you. We need an explanation."

Mr. Thompson's smile faltered, his eyes flickering with something that might have been fear. "I don't know what you're talking about," he said, his tone defensive. "I've always been on your side."

Alyssa stepped forward, holding up the incriminating document. "This transaction," she said, her voice firm. "It links your account to one of Whitewood's shell companies. Explain this."

Mr. Thompson's eyes darted around the room, as if seeking an escape. "You have to understand," he said, his voice tinged with desperation. "They threatened my family. I had no choice."

Dr. Philosopher's expression softened slightly, but his resolve remained firm. "There's was a choice, but now, you need to help us. We need to dismantle this network, and we can't do it alone."

Reluctantly, Mr. Thompson agreed to cooperate, providing them with valuable information about the remaining elements of Whitewood's network. His betrayal cut deep, but his assistance was crucial in their fight to secure Crestwood's future.

As they left Mr. Thompson's home, Alyssa felt a mix of relief and sorrow. They had uncovered another layer of deceit, but the cost had been high. Trust, once broken, was difficult to rebuild.

Back at the safe house, they regrouped, integrating the latest information into their plans. They were closer than ever to dismantling Whitewood's network, but the path ahead was fraught with danger.

"We're making progress," Derek said, his voice filled with determination. "But we can't let our guard down. There are still threats out there."

Evan nodded, his eyes steely with resolve. "We'll finish this. For Crestwood, and for everyone who's put their trust in us."

CHAPTER XXV

A Blood-Soaked Warning

Tension hung in the air like a thick fog in Crestwood as the team tirelessly worked to dismantle Whitewood's operations. Every new discovery revealed the breadth of his influence, and with each step forward, the threat seemed to grow. Unbeknownst to them, Whitewood was preparing a brutal reminder of his reach.

One evening, as they gathered at the safe house to review their findings, a knock at the door disrupted their focus. Derek opened it to find a local courier holding a package. "Delivery for Dr. Philosopher," the courier said, handing over the small, plain box.

Dr. Philosopher took the package with a frown. As he opened it, his expression shifted from confusion to horror. Inside was a blood-stained note with a chilling message: "Your efforts are futile. Stop now, or more will die."

Alyssa's face went pale as she read the note. "This is Whitewood's doing," she said, her voice barely above a whisper. "He's sending us a message."

Evan clenched his fists, anger flashing in his eyes. "We can't let him scare us into stopping," he said defiantly. "We have to keep pushing forward."

Derek, his eyes scanning the room, added, "We need to find out who the victim is and why Whitewood targeted them. This could be a clue to his next move."

Their investigation led them to the outskirts of town, where the body of a local businessperson, Mr. Grey, was discovered. The scene was gruesome, a stark reminder of Whitewood's ruthlessness. Mr. Grey had been an outspoken supporter of the team's efforts, providing financial backing and resources. His murder was a clear message: anyone who stood with them was a target.

Alyssa knelt beside the body; her eyes filled with determination. "We need to find out everything we can about his recent activities," she said. "Someone must have seen or heard something."

They spent the next few days interviewing neighbors, employees, and anyone who had been in contact with Mr. Grey. Gradually, a picture began to emerge. Mr. Grey had been meeting with several individuals, trying to rally more support for the team's cause. One name kept coming up: a man named Thatcher, known for his shady dealings and connections to Whitewood's network.

"We need to find Thatcher," Dr. Philosopher said, his voice filled with urgency. "He could be the key to uncovering Whitewood's next move."

Their search for Thatcher led them to a run-down tavern on the edge of town. The dimly lit interior was filled with unsavory characters, each one a potential threat. Alyssa, Derek, Evan, and Dr. Philosopher moved cautiously, their eyes scanning the room for any sign of their target.

It didn't take long to spot him. Thatcher was sitting in a corner booth, a nervous energy about him. As they approached, he tried to slip away, but Evan grabbed him by the arm, forcing him back into his seat.

"We need to talk," Alyssa said, her tone leaving no room for argument. "You've been meeting with Mr. Grey. What do you know about his murder?"

Thatcher's eyes darted around the room, sweat beading on his forehead. "I don't know anything," he stammered. "I was just doing business."

Derek leaned in, his voice low and menacing. "We know you're connected to Whitewood. If you don't start talking, things are going to get very unpleasant for you."

The fear in Thatcher's eyes was palpable. "Alright, alright," he said, his voice shaking. "I'll tell you what I know. Whitewood is planning something big. He's consolidating power, bringing in more weapons and men. Mr. Grey found out and tried to warn you. That's why he was killed."

Dr. Philosopher's eyes narrowed. "Where is Whitewood hiding? Where are these weapons coming from?"

Thatcher hesitated, glancing around nervously. "There's a shipment coming in tomorrow night," he finally said. "At the old docks. That's all I know, I swear."

Satisfied with the information, the team left the tavern, their minds already racing with plans. They knew the docks would be heavily guarded, but it was their best chance to strike at the heart of Whitewood's operations.

"We need to be prepared," Alyssa said as they returned to the safe house. "This could be our only shot at stopping him."

CHAPTER XXVI

Its Over...Or is it?

The victory at the docks gave the team a moment of triumph, but the weight of their mission quickly settled back upon them. Whitewood was still at large, and his network, though fractured, was far from destroyed. The murder of Mr. Grey had shown them the lengths Whitewood was willing to go, and they knew more bloodshed was inevitable if they didn't act swiftly.

Alyssa stood at the safe house window, watching the sun rise over Crestwood. Her mind raced with thoughts of their next steps. Dr. Phil approached, a concerned look on his face. "We need to stay ahead of him," he said, his voice breaking the silence. "We can't let him regroup and retaliate."

Derek and Evan joined them, their expressions mirroring the gravity of the situation. "We have to find Whitewood before he finds us," Derek said. "But where do we start? He's not going to make it easy."

Evan tapped the map laid out on the table. "We need to track his movements, find his safe houses, his supply lines. Anything that can lead us to him."

Alyssa nodded. "We should split up and cover more ground. Dr. Phil and I will take the eastern part of the town, Derek and Evan, you cover the west."

With a plan in place, they gathered their gear and set out. The town was eerily quiet, the recent chaos leaving an air of uncertainty. As they moved through the streets, they kept their eyes and ears open, searching for any sign of Whitewood or his operatives.

Dr. Phil and Alyssa made their way to an old warehouse district, a place known for its shadows and secrets. They questioned workers, vendors, anyone who might have seen something unusual. Hours passed with little success until a nervous dockworker finally spoke up.

"I saw some men loading crates into a van late last night," he said, his voice barely above a whisper. "Didn't recognize them, but they were definitely not from around here. They went north."

Alyssa's eyes lit up with a mix of hope and determination. "Thank you," she said, slipping the man a few bills. "Stay safe."

Meanwhile, Derek and Evan were having their own share of luck. At a rundown bar on the west side, they found a patron who claimed to have overheard a conversation about a hideout in the forest outside of town. "They were talking about meeting up there, something about a final stand," the man slurred, clearly inebriated but truthful.

As night fell, the team regrouped at the safe house to share their findings. The pieces of the puzzle were starting to come together. Whitewood's men were on the move, and the forest hideout seemed like the perfect place for him to regroup and plan his next move.

"We have to move quickly," Alyssa said, urgently in her voice. "If we wait, we might lose him again."

With their path set, they gathered their supplies and headed towards the forest. The air grew colder as they ventured deeper, the trees casting long, ominous shadows in the moonlight. Their senses were heightened, every rustle and snap putting them on edge.

As they approached the suspected hideout, they could see the glow of a campfire through the trees. The sounds of murmured conversations and the clinking of bottles reached their ears. They crept closer, staying low and moving silently.

Peering through the underbrush, they saw a group of men gathered around the fire. Whitewood was there, his figure unmistakable even in the dim light. He was speaking in deep tones, his voice carrying an edge of authority and menace.

"This is our last stand," Whitewood said, his tone leaving no room for dissent. "We will strike hard and fast, and we will reclaim what is ours."

Dr. Phil motioned for the group to spread out, signaling a coordinated approach. They moved into position, each taking careful aim. The tension was palpable, the moment stretched taut as a bowstring.

On Dr. Phil's signal, they sprang into action. The clearing erupted in chaos as gunfire and shouts filled the air. Whitewood's men scrambled to defend themselves, but the team's precision and determination gave them the upper hand.

During the battle, Alyssa spotted Whitewood trying to slip away. She pursued him through the trees, her heart pounding in her chest. She couldn't let him escape, not this time.

They reached a small clearing where Whitewood turned to face her, a cruel smile on his lips. "You think you can stop me?" he taunted, raising his weapon.

Alyssa didn't hesitate. She fired, her shot finding its mark. Whitewood staggered; the shock evident on his face. He fell to the ground, his reign of terror finally ended.

Breathing heavily, Alyssa stood over him, the weight of the moment sinking in. The rest of the team soon joined her, their expressions a mix of relief and exhaustion.

"It's over," Dr. Phil said, placing a hand on her shoulder. "You did it."

Alyssa nodded; her eyes fixed on Whitewood's lifeless body. "We did it," she corrected, looking at her brothers and their allies. "Together."

As dawn broke over the forest, they made their way back to Crestwood, the promise of a new beginning ahead of them.

"Something's not right."

CHAPTER XXVII

The Deceptive Victory

The victory over Whitewood had brought a temporary sense of peace to Crestwood. The town's people cautiously emerged from their homes, smiling with relief at the sight of Alyssa and her team. They were hailed as heroes, their courage and determination celebrated by grateful residents. But amidst the accolades, Alyssa couldn't shake the feeling that something was amiss. The ease with which they had captured Whitewood seemed too convenient, too orchestrated.

Back at the safe house, the team gathered to debrief and plan their next moves. As they discussed the night's events, Alyssa's phone buzzed unexpectedly. She glanced at the screen to see an anonymous message: "Did you really think it would be that simple?"

Showing the message to Dr. Phil, her closest advisor, they exchanged worried glances. "It could be a bluff," Dr. Phil suggested, but uncertainty lingered in his voice. "We should confirm the body."

Returning to where Whitewood's body had been left, a tense silence greeted them. The clearing felt eerily quiet as they approached the figure lying on the ground. Dr. Phil knelt beside it, examining closely. After a moment, he looked up, his face drained of color.

"This isn't Whitewood," he stated gravely. "It's a decoy, a high-quality mask disguising someone else."

Alyssa's heart sank. "If this isn't Whitewood, then where is he?" she asked, the dread palpable in her voice.

"We've been played," Alyssa concluded bitterly. "Whitewood orchestrated this deception to divert us while he regroups."

Dr. Phil nodded grimly. "He's always been steps ahead of us. Now we need to find out where he's hiding and put an end to this once and for all."

Their earlier victories now seemed fragile against the backdrop of looming uncertainty. The town, still reeling from recent turmoil, braced itself for the possibility of Whitewood's return.

As they deliberated their next moves, anxious whispers spread among the townspeople outside the safe house. Fear and uncertainty permeated the air. Recognizing the need to restore calm and maintain their credibility, the team dispersed to reassure residents and gather any intelligence that could lead them to Whitewood.

Days turned into an agonizing search for Whitewood's whereabouts. Every lead they pursued turned out to be a dead end, frustrating their efforts. Then, a breakthrough came with an intercepted communication from one of Whitewood's associates.

"He's hiding in the old mines outside of town," the message revealed. "He's planning something big."

With newfound determination, Alyssa and her team geared up for their next move. They approached the mines cautiously, aware that Whitewood could be expecting them. Inside the cold, damp tunnels, tension mounted as they ventured deeper, alert for any sign of danger.

Voices ahead alerted them to Whitewood's presence. They crept closer, stealthily observing him and his inner circle discussing their next operation. Alyssa's pulse quickened. This was their chance.

"We need to catch him off guard," Dr. Phil whispered, his eyes never leaving Whitewood.

They devised a plan to divide their forces: one group would create a distraction while the others would flank Whitewood's position from behind. Positioned and ready, nerves were taut, knowing one misstep could ruin everything.

Explosions echoed through the tunnels as the distraction team set off charges near the entrance, drawing Whitewood's attention. Alyssa and Dr. Phil led the flanking team through the labyrinthine passages, silently navigating to avoid detection.

Reaching a vantage point, they saw Whitewood and his guards ahead. With a silent signal, they launched their assault. The guards were caught off guard, unable to mount effective resistance against the well-coordinated attack.

Alyssa and Dr. Phil closed in on Whitewood, who turned to face them with a mixture of fury and disbelief. "You again?" he sneered, reaching for his weapon.

"It's over, Whitewood," Alyssa declared firmly, her resolve unwavering.

A fierce struggle ensued, reverberating through the caverns. Whitewood fought desperately, but the odds were against him. In a decisive moment, Dr. Phil disarmed him, leaving him defeated and vulnerable.

As Whitewood lay on the ground, subdued, and surrounded, the team breathed a collective sigh of relief. The threat that had haunted Crestwood for so long was finally neutralized.

Sirens blared in the distance as law enforcement arrived. Whitewood was apprehended, his reign of terror coming to a humiliating end. The townspeople, weary but relieved, emerged from their homes to witness the conclusion of their ordeal.

Amidst the chaos of the arrest, Alyssa found a moment of quiet reflection. She looked at her brothers and Dr. Phil, their faces worn but also filled with pride. Together, they confronted their fears and emerged victorious.

As Whitewood was led away, Crestwood began to heal once more. Though scars from his tyranny lingered, a renewed sense of unity and resilience began to take hold in the community.

And just as they reached home, ready to relax from their amazing journey, a faint buzz broke the silence—Alyssa's Phone. A video message flickered to life, revealing Whitewood's chilling grin. 'You think it's over?' he taunted.

"Wait until you meet *Alex*."

"Who's Alex?"

Stay tuned for the next thrilling book.
The adventure continues soon!
:)

About The Author

Nitya Malapil was born in mid-2007, Dubai, UAE. She lives in Dubai, and this is her first novel.

She is a bibliophile, a music fan, and a high school graduate. With the help of her friends and teacher, she earned up the interest of drafting a book to put out her imaginations to the world. You can find more about her on her website. https://sites.google.com/view/nitya238